STRAWBERRY
DRESS ESCAPE

STRAWBERRY DRESS ESCAPE

by **CRESCENT DRAGONWAGON**
pictures by **LILLIAN HOBAN**

CHARLES SCRIBNER'S SONS, NEW YORK

1 3 5 7 9 11 13 15 17 19 RD/C 20 18 16 14 12 10 8 6 4 2

Printed in the United States of America
Library of Congress Catalog Card Number 74-14074
ISBN 0-684-13912-X

Nothing ends
but everything changes
Love never disperses
but is transmuted:
crumbly humus
new gardens bloom—
M.S., this is for you.

Emily was sitting in class.

It was almost summer and school would soon be out.

It was boring in class.

Emily could hardly understand Teacher's voice.

She could only hear it rising and falling.

Teacher made numbers on the blackboard.

The room was dusty.

Emily felt like choking.

It was a hot, hot day.

She must look at the numbers on the board
with her hands folded.
All the children must look at the
numbers on the board with
their hands folded.

The windows in the schoolroom were open.

Emily could hear bees buzzing outside.

She could smell honeysuckle.

Emily stood up and slipped away.

Nobody noticed she had gone.

Teacher went on making sounds about numbers.

Emily skipped down the dirt road to a field.
It was her field.
She put her arms up and flew around the
edges of it three times.

As she looked down she saw
  green grass,
  yellow and white daisies,
  several honeysuckle bushes,
  and her pet goat, Emerald,
  who was eating grass.

It was very hot.
As she flew, Emily sang a song.
 "sky is tree
   both-a are me
   it is hot
   i am not
   i escaped
   i am shaped
   like a bee—
   i am free!"

"Hullo, Emerald," Emily said, as she lit on the ground.
"Have you some sweet milk for me?" Emerald was brown
and white with a wise beard and bright, green eyes.
She had a silver bell around her neck.
  "Maaaaaah,"
she said, and her bell rang softly under the sun.
Emerald winked one of her green eyes.

Emily sat on the ground with her legs x-ed like
an Indian under her skirt.
Her skirt had little strawberries growing all
over it, and it was long enough to carry things in.

Then Emily reached up under Emerald and went
    squueezepull! squueezepull!
Milk foamed out in a thin stream onto the ground—
    squueezepull!
Emily sent a stream of sweet, warm milk
right into her mouth.
  "A most kind goat is Emerald.
    She likes to have her udders pulled!
    Her eyes are green; her coat is spotted.
    We share a field with daisies dotted!"

Emily scratched Emerald behind the ears.
Then she walked over to the apple tree.
Under the apple tree was a basket with all
kinds of fruit in it:

    softripe cherries, purple-black
    soursweet apples, crisp
    and a pear that fit Emily's hand perfectly.

Emily put her mouth into the pear and leaned
over so the juice poured into the field.
The flavor of the pear whispered,
  "Ask the snake in the ring of mushrooms."
  "Ask the snake what?" Emily inquired, but the
pear replied only in grainy sweetness.

The snake in the ring of mushrooms was
striped black and yellow.
His dry body twisted and moved in her hand.
"Would you tell me?" asked Emily.

"I would suggesssssst ssssssskipping rrrrope,"
said the snake, and his tongue flicked in and out.
  "Snaketongue dance pass
    slither thru the wet, green grass."
And the snake moved away like Ss, so
quickly there was only time to
find the skipping rope with the
red handles that lay in the
grass in front of her.

Emily began to skip, but with
each skip, she seemed to move more slowly.
The rope went around her slowly and she seemed to
stay off the ground for the longest time.

When she came down she floated
like dandelion dust.
 "I feel so sleepy," she said.
Slowly Emily came down, slowly
she skipped through the rope,
slowly she floated up again.

"I'm so sleepy," Emily yawned. "This rope is telling
me I have skipped enough."
Emily folded the rope up and laid it under
some ferns near the ring of mushrooms.
    Slowly, slowly
all her moves were smooth and connected.
  "I feel like going to the center,"
and Emily ran, but every step was a long,
slow, light leap.

She came to the center of the field.
And there, in the very center of the field,
was a bed.

It had polished brass posts and
they shone brightly in the sun.
It had golden sheets, perfectly clean and smooth.
The top one was neatly folded half-back.
Emily hung up her strawberry dress on
one of the polished brass posts.
She untied her shoes and kicked them up into
the air where they became pigeons.

And as she climbed into the golden bed
and curled over on her side,
the pigeons came down next to her,
cooing softly with their heads under
their wings.

And they all three
went to sleep under the sun.

Crescent Dragonwagon is twenty-one years old. She was born in New York City and is the author of one previous book for children and three cookbooks. Her articles have appeared in *Seventeen, Organic Gardening and Farming* and *Cosmopolitan*. She now lives in Eureka Springs, Arkansas, where she cooks, gardens, reads, and studies astrology.

The warmth and good humor of Lillian Hoban's illustrations have made her one of the most popular and respected of children's book illustrators. Recently she has turned to writing as well. Some of her books are *Sugar Snow Spring* and *Arthur's Christmas Cookies.* Among the many books she has illustrated are *Rainy Day Together,* the "Frances" books, and *The Sorely Trying Day.*